and

Sleeping Beauty

As well as the Disney Classic Retellings, Narinder Dhami is the author of numerous books including *Angel Face*, *Animal Crackers* and *Annie's Game* (all shortlisted for awards). Her most recent success is the novel of the hit British comedy *Bend it Like Beckham*. Narinder lives in Cambridge.

PUFFIN BOOKS

Published by the Penguin Group
Penguin Books Ltd, 80 Strand, London WC2R 0RL, England
Penguin Group (USA), Inc., 375 Hudson Street, New York, New York 10014, USA
Penguin Books Australia Ltd, 250 Camberwell Road, Camberwell, Victoria 3124, Australia
Penguin Books Canada Ltd, 10 Alcorn Avenue, Toronto, Ontario, Canada M4V 3B2
Penguin Books India (P) Ltd, 11 Community Centre, Panchsheel Park, New Delhi – 110 017, India
Penguin Group (NZ), cnr Airborne and Rosedale Roads, Albany, Auckland 1310, New Zealand
Penguin Books (South Africa) (Pty) Ltd, 24 Sturdee Avenue, Rosebank 2196, South Africa

Penguin Books Ltd, Registered Offices: 80 Strand, London WC2R 0RL, England

Cinderella first published 2003
Sleeping Beauty first published 2003
First published in one volume 2004

1

Copyright © Disney Enterprises, Inc., 2003, 2004
All rights reserved

Set in 16/25 Cochin
Made and printed in England by Clays Ltd, St Ives plc

Except in the United States of America, this book is sold subject to the condition that it
shall not, by way of trade or otherwise, be lent, re-sold, hired out, or otherwise circulated
without the publisher's prior consent in any form of binding or cover other than that in
which it is published and without a similar condition including this condition being
imposed on the subsequent purchaser

British Library Cataloguing in Publication Data
A CIP catalogue record for this book is available from the British Library

ISBN 0–141–31852–X

Cinderella

and Sleeping Beauty

Narinder Dhami

PUFFIN

Contents

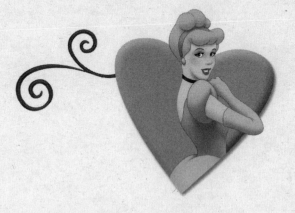

Cinderella

Contents

Chapter One

'Wake up, Cinderella!'

Cinderella yawned and opened her eyes. She smiled to see two bluebirds perched upon her pillow, singing sweetly.

'Oh,' she sighed, 'I was having such a lovely dream too.'

Her face fell as she considered the day that lay ahead of her: cooking, cleaning, washing, ironing, running around after her stepmother, Lady Tremaine, her two stepsisters, Drizella and Anastasia, and their fat, spoilt cat, Lucifer.

And whatever I do, it's never enough, Cinderella thought sadly. They always want me to do more.

Her thoughts flew back to when her father was alive. Then she had been loved and given everything she wanted. But her father had died soon after marrying her stepmother and now Cinderella was nothing more than a slave in the big, beautiful house where she had been brought up. Sometimes she felt that her only friends were the animals who lived in the house and out in the barnyard: the birds, the mice, her old horse and her dog, Bruno, who had been a present from her father many years ago, when she was a little girl.

The birds chirped again, looking at Cinderella with bright eyes.

'No, I can't tell you what my dream was about!' She smiled. 'If I tell you, it won't come true.' Her eyes grew dreamy and she began to sing to herself: 'Have faith in your dreams, and someday the dream that you wish will come true …'

BONG!

'Oh, that clock!' Cinderella ran over to the window and leaned out to look at the clock tower of the palace in the distance. 'Even he orders me around!' She smiled. 'Well, there's one thing they can't do. They can't order me to stop dreaming.'

Cinderella washed and dressed, still singing to herself. Then she hurried down the stairs to the next landing, opening the curtains on her way. She slipped into her stepmother's bedroom, which was still in darkness. Next to the bed slept a fat, black cat.

'Here, kitty,' Cinderella called softly.

Lucifer stared disdainfully at Cinderella. Then he curled up again and closed his eyes.

'Lucifer,' Cinderella whispered. 'Come here.'

This time the cat got grumpily to his feet and stalked out of the door, tail waving.

'It's not my idea to feed you first in the mornings,' Cinderella said, hurrying down the stairs. 'It's Stepmother's orders.' And Cinderella knew what would happen if she didn't do as she was told …

Down in the kitchen Bruno was asleep on the rug. Cinderella loved her dog dearly, but it was difficult to stop him chasing Lucifer, especially when the cat annoyed him. Lucifer was strolling round and round poor Bruno now, deliberately tickling the dog's nose with his fluffy tail.

'You'd better learn to like cats, Bruno,' Cinderella told him, 'or you'll lose your nice warm bed. And I'll lose you.'

Then she jumped as the bells on the wall began to ring loudly.

'Cinderella!' called a cross voice. 'Cinderella!'

Chapter Two

'All right,' Cinderella sighed. 'I'm coming.'

She rushed across the kitchen and began placing cups and saucers on three trays.

'Cinderella!'

Quickly, she poured hot water into a teapot. Then she picked up the trays, balancing them carefully in her arms, and hurried out of the kitchen as fast as she dared.

'Good morning, Drizella,' she said cheerfully, pushing open the door of the first bedroom. 'Did you sleep well?'

'Huh!' Drizella sniffed, and snatched a tray. 'As if you cared! Take that ironing –' she pointed at a basket heaped with crumpled clothes – 'and have it ready in an hour.'

'Yes, Drizella,' replied Cinderella. She picked up the basket and went into the second bedroom.

'Well, it's about time!' Anastasia grumbled. 'Don't forget my mending.' She took one of the trays and pointed at a basket full of clothes. 'And don't take all day about it either!'

'Yes, Anastasia,' replied Cinderella, and, carrying the two baskets, went to her stepmother's room.

'Come in, child.' Her stepmother was a tall, thin, elegant woman with a pale, cruel face.

'Good morning, Stepmother,' Cinderella said, handing her a breakfast tray.

'Pick up the laundry and get on with your duties,' replied her stepmother coldly.

Cinderella hurried out with the three baskets. She had just reached the top of the stairs when she heard a bloodcurdling scream from Anastasia's bedroom: 'AAAAHHHHHHH!'

She dashed back down the landing. Just as she reached the room, the door was flung open and Anastasia stood there glaring at her.

'You did it!' she shrieked.

Cinderella looked puzzled. Still squealing, Anastasia pushed her aside and ran into her mother's bedroom.

'Mother!' she wailed.

Drizella appeared in the doorway of her room. 'Now what did you do?' she snapped at Cinderella.

'She put it there!' Anastasia was screaming. 'A big ugly mouse! Under my teacup!'

Cinderella looked startled. Why had one of her tiny friends been hiding under the teacup? Perhaps the cat had been chasing him. She swung round and saw Lucifer sitting on the landing, his paws tucked neatly in front of him. He looked very smug.

'All right, Lucifer,' Cinderella said, as the cat stared innocently at her, 'what happened to the mouse?' She lifted the cat up and a fat little mouse rolled out from under his paws. 'Oh, you poor thing!' Cinderella cried.

Looking terrified, the mouse dashed off across the floor and disappeared down a hole.

'Cinderella!' Her stepmother's voice rang out.

Cinderella hurried into the bedroom. Anastasia and Drizella stood smirking in the doorway as she passed them.

'Are you going to get it,' Anastasia whispered.

'Shut the door, Cinderella,' her stepmother ordered.

Cinderella closed the door, knowing that her stepsisters would be listening at the keyhole. Her stepmother sat in bed, her eyes bright and hard. Lucifer jumped on to the quilt, purring smugly, and settled down.

'Oh, please,' Cinderella began anxiously, 'you don't think that I –'

'Hold your tongue.' Her stepmother pulled the breakfast tray closer. 'It seems you have time on your hands for playing vicious practical jokes.'

'But –'

'Silence!' Lady Tremaine reached for the teapot. 'But perhaps we can put that time to better use.'

Lucifer smirked.

'Now let me see,' her stepmother went

on, pouring cream into her tea. 'There are the carpets to be cleaned, and all the windows too. And, oh yes –' she smiled an evil smile – 'the tapestries to be washed.'

'But I just finished –'

'Do them again!' her stepmother thundered. 'Then scrub the terrace and clean the halls. And –' her smile deepened – 'see that Lucifer gets his bath.'

Chapter Three

'It's high time he got married and settled down!'

The Duke ducked as a crown flew across the room towards him. It sailed through the palace window, scattering the pigeons on the ledge.

'Yes, Your Majesty,' the Duke agreed quickly. 'But we must be patient.'

An ink bottle splattered against the wall behind him.

'I AM patient!' roared the King

furiously. 'But I'm not getting any younger. I want to see my grandchildren before I go.' He stared gloomily at the pictures of his son, the Prince, on the wall. 'He's got all these silly romantic ideas!'

'Now, Your Majesty,' the Duke said soothingly, 'maybe if we just left the Prince to find his own wife –'

'No, I have a much better idea!' the King retorted. 'We'll hold a ball here at the palace. And we'll invite all the most eligible ladies in the kingdom.' He laughed. 'Soft lights, romantic music. It can't fail!'

'V-very well, Sire,' the Duke stammered. 'I'll arrange the ball for –'

'Tonight!' the King broke in. 'And see

that every girl in the kingdom is there.
I'm going to make sure my son finds a
wife! Understand?'

Cinderella scrubbed the marble floor. She
was already tired out, but she was only
halfway through cleaning the lower hall.
In the distance she could hear her
stepmother at the piano as Drizella and
Anastasia practised their singing.

Cinderella sat back on her heels and
rested for a moment. Then she gasped as
Lucifer padded through the hall, leaving
dirty pawprints on the newly washed
floor.

'Oh, you mean old thing!' Cinderella
exclaimed. She jumped to her feet just as
there was a knock at the door.

'Open in the name of the King,' called
an important-sounding voice.

Cinderella hurried to open the door.
A messenger bowed and handed her
a letter.

'An urgent message from His Imperial
Majesty!' he announced.

'Whatever can this be?' Cinderella
thought, staring at the letter as she went
over to the music room.

Her stepmother swung round from the
piano to glare at her. 'I warned you never
to interrupt us,' she snapped.

'But this came from the palace,'
Cinderella explained, holding up the
letter.

'The palace!' shrieked Drizella.
She rushed across to Cinderella and

snatched the letter from her.

'Let me have it!' Anastasia roared, grabbing it from her sister.

'I'll read it.' Cinderella's stepmother took the letter and opened it. 'Well!' A satisfied smile spread across her thin face. 'There is to be a ball, in honour of the Prince!'

'The Prince!' sighed Anastasia and Drizella happily.

'And every girl in the kingdom is to attend,' Cinderella's stepmother went on.

'Oh!' Cinderella clasped her hands in delight. 'That means I can go too!'

Drizella burst into mocking laughter. 'Her dancing with the Prince! Ha ha!'

'I'd be honoured, Your Highness! Would you mind holding my broom?'

Anastasia spluttered, giggling.

'It says every girl in the kingdom,' Cinderella pointed out.

Her stepmother glanced at the letter. 'So it does,' she said silkily. 'I see no reason why you can't go, if you get all your work done. And if you can find something suitable to wear.'

'I'm sure I can,' Cinderella agreed happily. 'Thank you, Stepmother!' And she ran lightly from the room.

'Mother!' Drizella moaned. 'Do you realize what you just said?'

'Of course,' her mother replied, with a wry smile. 'I said if.'

Chapter Four

'Isn't it lovely?' Cinderella whirled round the room, holding a dress against her, as her friends the birds and the mice watched. 'It was my mother's.'

Then she frowned. 'Well, maybe it is a little old-fashioned. But I'll fix that.' Humming happily to herself, Cinderella fetched her sewing basket. 'I'll have to shorten the sleeves and I'll need a sash. Oh, and I'll have to change the collar. And –'

'Cinderella!'

Cinderella sighed. 'Oh, now what do they want?'

'Cinderella!'

'Oh well, my dress will just have to wait,' Cinderella murmured, hurrying over to the door. 'All right, I'm coming!'

For the rest of the day Cinderella didn't have a minute to herself. Her stepmother kept finding jobs for her to do: 'Cinderella, sweep the front steps. Cinderella, clean the stove. Cinderella, make us some tea.' Drizella and Anastasia were very excited about the ball, and Cinderella ran up and down the stairs fetching and carrying for them a hundred times. She had to iron their dresses, tie their ribbons and clean their shoes. With a heavy heart, she realized that she wasn't going to have time to prepare her own dress. She wouldn't be able to go to the ball.

As night began to fall, Cinderella was standing at one of the upstairs windows, watching while the carriage swept up to the door. How I wish I was going to the ball too, she thought longingly, before going to her stepmother's room.

'The carriage is here,' Cinderella announced.

Her stepmother raised her eyebrows. 'You're not ready, child.'

'I'm not going,' Cinderella replied sadly.

A hint of a smile played around her stepmother's lips. 'Not going? Oh, what a shame.'

Trying not to cry, Cinderella rushed to her room. It was dark and empty. She wandered over to the window and gazed out at the brightly lit palace in the distance. 'I suppose it would be quite dull and boring,' she said bravely to herself. 'Oh, and completely wonderful ...'

Suddenly light flooded her room. Cinderella gasped as she turned to see a beautiful dress before her. It was her dress, and it looked wonderful. The sleeves had been shortened, the collar had been changed, it had a new sash and it had been trimmed with ribbons and beads. As Cinderella stared, her friends the mice and the birds watched her happily.

'Oh!' Cinderella couldn't believe her

eyes. 'You did all this? How can I ever thank you?'

Quickly, she pulled off her rags and slipped into the new dress. It fitted her perfectly. Then she ran down the stairs, catching up with her stepmother and stepsisters in the lower hall as they made their way to the carriage.

'Please wait for me!' Cinderella called, feeling as if her heart would burst with happiness.

Her stepmother and stepsisters stared in amazement at the beautiful dress.

'Mother, she can't come!' Drizella and Anastasia hissed furiously.

'Girls, I never go back on my word.' Their mother stepped forward and fingered the beads round Cinderella's neck. 'These look very nice, don't you think?'

'No, I don't!' Drizella snapped sulkily. Then her eyes narrowed. 'Why, they're MY beads!' She reached out and pulled them roughly from Cinderella's neck.

'And that's my sash!' shrieked Anastasia, grabbing it and tearing Cinderella's skirt.

'And that's my ribbon!' Drizella ripped it off and the dress tore again.

Cinderella gasped and covered her face with her hands. Her dress was ruined.

'Girls, that's quite enough.' Their mother ushered Drizella and Anastasia outside, smiling triumphantly. 'Goodnight, Cinderella.'

Chapter Five

Sobbing as if her heart would break,
Cinderella ran out of the house and
across the garden. She sank down on to a
bench, still crying. Now her dreams
would never come true …

'My dreams are no use at all,' she
sobbed, as Bruno, the mice and her other
animal friends watched her anxiously.
'There's nothing left to believe in any
more.'

Suddenly someone began to stroke her

hair. 'You don't really believe that, my dear,' said a kindly voice.

Cinderella looked up. Through her tears she could make out an elderly woman with a smiling face and twinkling blue eyes. Cinderella had never seen her before, but she liked her immediately.

'Oh, but I do mean it!' she gulped.

'Nonsense, child,' said the woman. 'If you really meant it, I wouldn't be here – and here I am! So dry those tears. You can't go to the ball looking like that.'

'But I'm not –' Cinderella began.

'Of course you are,' her new friend replied briskly. 'Now what in the world did I do with my magic wand?' She began to look around her.

'Magic wand?' Cinderella repeated,

wondering if she'd heard correctly. 'Why, then, you must be –'

'Your fairy godmother, of course.' Cinderella's fairy godmother frowned. 'Now where is that wand? Oh, I forgot – I put it away!' She waved her hand and the wand appeared out of nowhere. 'The first thing we need is a pumpkin.'

Cinderella's eyes opened wide. 'A pumpkin?'

Her fairy godmother glanced around the garden and picked out a fine, fat orange pumpkin. She tapped it with her wand and, with a whirl of magic sparks, the pumpkin turned instantly into a glittering golden carriage.

'Oh, it's beautiful!' Cinderella gasped.

'Now we need four horses.'

Her fairy godmother looked down at the group of mice watching timidly. With one flash of her wand, they became elegant white horses with long flowing manes.

'You can't go to the ball without a coachman,' she went on.

She waved her wand at Cinderella's old horse, who was standing in the yard, and the next moment there was a coachman in a smart uniform to drive her to the palace.

'And now the finishing touch ...'

At her fairy godmother's words, Cinderella looked down hopefully at her tattered dress.

'Bruno!' Cinderella's fairy godmother turned to the old dog. 'You'll be footman tonight!'

In the blink of an eye, Bruno was wearing the same smart uniform as the coachman.

'Well, hop in, my dear.' Cinderella's fairy godmother ushered her towards the coach. 'We can't waste any time.'

'B-but,' Cinderella stammered, 'don't you think my dress –'

Her fairy godmother looked startled. 'Good heavens!' she cried, taking a closer look at the torn frock. 'You can't go in that!' She lifted her wand and magic sparks whirled and whooshed around Cinderella.

'Oh!' Cinderella gasped, staring down at the dazzling blue dress and high-heeled shoes she now wore. She looked so different, she felt sure not even her stepsisters would recognize her. 'And glass slippers too! It's like a dream come true!'

Her fairy godmother looked grave. 'But like all dreams, I'm afraid this one can't last forever, my dear. You must be home by midnight. At the stroke of twelve, the spell will be broken and everything will be as it was before!'

Chapter Six

The castle ballroom was filled with people dressed in their finest clothes. Candles cast a soft light as musicians played quietly in the background. At one end of the long room stood the handsome Prince and his father. The King had insisted that the Prince greet every single guest himself.

'The Princess Frederica,' announced the herald.

The Prince bowed politely at the girl,

who then moved down the ballroom as another took her place.

'Miss Augustine Dubois,' the herald went on.

Looking anxious, the King turned to the Duke, who was at his side. 'He doesn't seem interested in any of them!' he muttered.

At that moment the Prince caught his father's eye and yawned.

The King frowned. 'I can't understand it,' he groaned. 'Surely there must be one ...'

At that moment, her eyes shining, Cinderella entered the ballroom. Everyone turned to look at her as she walked gracefully down the length of the room, her dress shimmering in the candlelight. She could hardly believe that she was here, at the palace, at last!

'Drizella and Anastasia Tremaine, daughters of Lady Tremaine,' announced the herald.

The Prince looked taken aback as Drizella and Anastasia hurried forward, but bowed politely.

The King took one look at the sisters and groaned. 'I give up!' he muttered.

'Never mind, Your Majesty,' said the Duke comfortingly. 'It was bound to fail.'

Suddenly the Prince spotted Cinderella. Their eyes met. Cinderella smiled shyly and immediately the Prince hurried past Drizella and Anastasia towards her and took her hand. Together they began to dance.

'Bound to fail, eh?' laughed the King,

pointing at the Prince and Cinderella. 'What do you think of that, then?'

The Prince and Cinderella were waltzing round the room, smiling at each other. They had eyes for no one else. Meanwhile Drizella and Anastasia watched furiously.

'Who is she, Mother?' Drizella wailed.

'I've never seen her before,' their mother replied thoughtfully, 'but she certainly seems familiar.'

Cinderella and the Prince danced on. Then they walked in the garden and talked, just the two of them, and Cinderella felt as if she was living in a beautiful dream. As the Prince bent to kiss her for the first time, she closed her eyes.

BONG!

'Oh!' Cinderella gasped. 'It's midnight!'

'Yes.' The Prince looked puzzled. 'But –'

'I must go! Goodbye!' And with that, Cinderella picked up her skirts and ran off through the palace.

'But I don't even know your name!' the Prince cried as he hurried after her.

Cinderella didn't dare to stop. She flew down the steps towards the waiting carriage. As she did so, one of her glass slippers came loose and fell off. She turned to go back for it, just as the Duke came dashing after her.

'Wait a moment, Miss!' he called.

With no time to spare, Cinderella left

the slipper where it was and jumped into the carriage. The coachman shook the reins and the horses galloped off as the clock continued to chime the midnight hour.

Chapter Seven

'I'm sorry, Your Majesty,' the Duke explained nervously, 'but all we could find was this glass slipper.'

The King bounced out of bed, looking furious. 'What! You mean you don't know her name or where she lives?'

The Duke shook his head. 'But the Prince is determined to marry her, Sire,' he went on hastily. He held up the glittering glass slipper. 'He swears that he'll marry none but the girl this slipper fits.'

'He said that, did he?' The King looked pleased. 'This slipper might fit any number of girls in my kingdom. We'll find him a wife yet!' He turned to the Duke. 'Try this slipper on every girl in the land,' he ordered, 'and if the shoe fits, bring her to me!'

Shortly afterwards, the King's messengers were busy going around the city posting notices everywhere. These announced that every unmarried girl had to try on the glass slipper. The girl it fitted would be the Prince's bride. Everyone was very excited. People stood in the streets reading the notices and talking to each other, wondering who the mysterious owner of the glass slipper could be.

Cinderella's father died soon after marrying her stepmother.

Cinderella was nothing more than a slave.

'They can't order me to stop dreaming.'

'An urgent message from His Imperial Majesty!'

'There is to be a ball in honour of the Prince!'

'Isn't it lovely? It was my mother's!'

'It's like a dream come true!'

Together they began to dance.

With no time to spare, Cinderella left the slipper
where it was.

'If one girl can be found whom the slipper fits, that girl will
be the Prince's bride!'

The Duke slid the glass slipper on to
Cinderella's slender foot.

Cinderella and her Prince lived happily ever after.

Lady Tremaine went out early to see what all the fuss was about. She soon came across one of the royal proclamations and rushed back home immediately.

'Cinderella!' she called sharply as she took off her cloak in the entrance hall. 'Where are my daughters?'

Cinderella came hurrying down the stairs. 'I think they're still in bed,' she replied.

'Well, don't just stand there,' her stepmother snapped. 'Bring up a breakfast tray at once.'

Lady Tremaine brushed past Cinderella and went upstairs into Drizella's bedroom. 'Get up,' she said, pulling the curtains as Drizella yawned and rubbed her eyes. 'We haven't a moment to lose.'

She rushed out and into Anastasia's room. 'Hurry now, get up,' she urged.

'Huh?' Anastasia mumbled from under the covers. 'Why?'

'Because he'll be here any minute!' her mother replied.

'Who will?' asked Drizella, shuffling into the room.

'The Duke!' Lady Tremaine told her. 'He's been looking for that girl all night.'

Cinderella was carrying the breakfast tray down the landing. Her eyes widened as she heard what her stepmother was saying.

'They say the Prince is madly in love with her!' Lady Tremaine went on.

'OH!' Cinderella was so startled, the

tray slipped from her hands. It crashed to the floor, and the cups and saucers broke into a thousand pieces.

Chapter Eight

'You clumsy little fool!' Lady Tremaine stalked out on to the landing to find Cinderella on her hands and knees picking up broken bits of crockery. 'Clear that up quickly, then help my daughters to dress.'

'What for?' Drizella moaned.

'If he's in love with that other girl, why should we even bother?' Anastasia demanded sulkily.

'Now, you two, listen to me,' said their

mother sternly. 'There is still a chance that one of you can marry him. No one, not even the Prince, knows who that girl is. The glass slipper is the only clue.'

Cinderella's heart leapt as she heard that. Quietly, she cleaned up the rest of the mess, listening hard.

'And if one girl can be found whom the slipper fits,' Lady Tremaine went on, 'that girl will be the Prince's bride.'

'His bride!' Cinderella repeated to herself.

Drizella and Anastasia looked thrilled. 'Cinderella, mend these clothes,' Anastasia ordered.

'No, iron my dress!' Drizella snapped.

As Cinderella stood there dreamily holding the tray, the sisters piled heaps of clothes upon it. Cinderella didn't even notice. She was thinking about her handsome Prince. She didn't even see the sharp glance her stepmother gave her.

'Wake up, stupid!' Drizella yelled at Cinderella.

'We've got to get dressed!' Anastasia roared.

'Yes.' Her eyes still dreamy, Cinderella glanced down at herself. 'Oh, yes, we must get dressed,' she agreed.

She pushed the clothes into Drizella's arms and walked off.

'Mother!' Drizella wailed. 'Did you see what she just did?'

'Quiet!' Lady Tremaine watched Cinderella waltzing down the landing. She was humming to herself. It was the same song that she and the Prince had danced to the night before.

Lady Tremaine's eyes narrowed. Now she knew the identity of the mysterious owner of the glass slipper. Quietly, she followed Cinderella along the landing.

Cinderella hurried into her room and began to comb her hair. For once she felt light-hearted and happy. Was it really possible that the Prince had fallen in love with her too?

Suddenly she glanced up and saw her stepmother reflected in the looking glass. The smile on Cinderella's face vanished as she watched Lady Tremaine whisk the key from the lock and pull the door tightly shut.

'Oh, no!' Cinderella gasped, rushing

across the room as she heard the key turn in the lock. 'You can't!'

Chapter Nine

Lady Tremaine ignored her cries. She slipped the key into her pocket and went back to her daughters, pleased with her deftness. However, she didn't notice that Cinderella's friends the mice had seen what she had done. Two of them sneaked downstairs after her, determined to get hold of that key and let Cinderella out.

'Mother!' Anastasia and Drizella were calling excitedly. 'He's here! He's here!'

A golden coach was drawing up

outside the house. Inside sat the Duke, holding the glass slipper on a velvet cushion. Drizella and Anastasia immediately rushed over to the mirror and began preening themselves.

'Oh, do I look all right?' Anastasia gasped. 'I'm so excited!'

'Girls!' Lady Tremaine held up her hand. 'Now remember. This is your last chance. Don't fail me.' She opened the door, and a footman stepped forward.

'His Grace, the Grand Duke,' he announced.

Lady Tremaine bowed. 'My lord,' she began, as the Duke entered the hall, 'may I present my daughters, Drizella and Anastasia.'

Anastasia and Drizella giggled and

curtsied.

'Why, that's my slipper!' Drizella announced loudly, as the footman held out the velvet cushion on which the glass slipper lay.

Anastasia glared at her. 'Well, I like that!' she snapped. 'It's my slipper!'

'Girls!' scolded their mother, as the footman looked rather nervous.

Meanwhile, one of the mice was climbing down into Lady Tremaine's pocket, with the other holding fast to his tail. The key was big and heavy, but at last they managed to pull it out. Immediately, they scampered off with it.

'We must get on with the fitting,' the Duke said.

Anastasia pushed Drizella out of the

way and sat down. 'There!' she exclaimed triumphantly as the footman slid the slipper on to her foot. 'I knew it was my slipper! It's exactly my size!'

The footman lifted her foot to show the Duke, and everyone could see that the slipper was sitting on only her toes. It was much too small for her.

'I don't understand it,' Anastasia mumbled crossly. 'It's always fitted perfectly before!'

The Duke pointed at Drizella. 'Now the next young lady.'

All this time Cinderella had been upstairs, kneeling by the door and sobbing quietly. Suddenly she heard squeaking. She looked through the keyhole and there were the two mice, huffing and puffing as they hauled the key up the stairs.

But then a shadow fell over the mice. It was Lucifer. Quick as a flash, the cat sprang towards them and trapped one of the mice as well as the key under an upturned bowl. Some of the other mice rushed to help, but Lucifer was too strong for them.

'Bruno!' Cinderella called desperately. 'Fetch Bruno!'

The dog was snoozing in the sunshine out in the yard. Quickly, Cinderella's friends the birds flew down and began to pull at his tail and ears, trying to wake him up.

Back inside the house, Drizella was getting ready to try on the glass slipper.

She grabbed it crossly from the footman, announcing, 'I'll do it myself,' and crammed her toes in. 'I'll make it fit!'

Her mother smiled as Drizella held out her foot. 'It fits!' she declared.

'It fits!' echoed the Duke.

But suddenly Drizella's foot burst out of the slipper, which flew up into the air, to be safely caught by the footman.

Meanwhile, the birds had managed to wake Bruno. He dashed into the house and up the stairs towards Cinderella's room. There he came nose-to-nose with Lucifer. He growled loudly. He'd been waiting for this day for a long time!

Looking scared, Lucifer backed right up to the window-ledge. As Bruno jumped towards him, Lucifer fell backwards and tumbled out of the window.

Downstairs, the Duke and the footman were now ready to leave.

'You are the only ladies of the house?' the Duke asked.

'There's no one else, Your Grace,' Lady Tremaine replied.

'Your Grace!' Cinderella called from the top of the stairs. 'May I try the slipper on, please?'

Chapter Ten

'Pay no attention to her!' Lady Tremaine snapped. 'It's only our kitchen maid.'

'Madam – my orders – every girl must try the slipper,' the Duke replied sternly.

Drizella and Anastasia looked on in disgust as Cinderella ran lightly down the stairs towards them, a happy smile on her face. The Duke took her hand and led her over to the chair, and the footman hurried across to her with the glass slipper.

Lady Tremaine looked slyly from left to right. Then she stuck out her cane, right in front of the footman. He gasped as he tripped and fell heavily. The slipper flew from the cushion, hit the floor and smashed into a million tiny slivers.

'Oh, no!' the Duke groaned, as Lady Tremaine smiled smugly. 'This is terrible! What will the King say?'

'But I have the other slipper!' Cinderella said.

She slipped her hand into her apron pocket and pulled out the identical shining slipper. Lady Tremaine was horror-struck, and Drizella and Anastasia were, for once, unable to say a word.

The Duke slid the glass slipper on to Cinderella's slender foot and, needless to say, it fitted perfectly.

So Cinderella and the Prince were reunited. And very soon afterwards their wedding took place at the castle. Everyone in the whole kingdom was invited to join in the celebrations, including Cinderella's friends the mice, the birds and Bruno. Everyone, that is, except her cruel stepmother and stepsisters. And, of course, Lucifer!

Sleeping Beauty

Contents

Chapter One

'Long live Princess Aurora! Long live
Princess Aurora!'

A large, colourful procession was
winding its way through the town
towards the castle. Soldiers in armour
trotted along on horseback, followed by
trumpeters and jugglers. Banners and
flags fluttered in the breeze, and the
townsfolk wore their best and brightest
clothes.

There was great excitement throughout

the land because at last a baby princess had been born. King Stefan and his Queen had longed for a child for many years and finally their wish had been granted. Now everyone had gathered to celebrate the arrival of little Princess Aurora.

Inside the castle, the throne room was teeming with people. The King and Queen were seated on their thrones, smiling proudly at their daughter, who lay sleeping peacefully in her cradle. Even a sudden blast of trumpets didn't wake her up.

A herald stepped forward and unrolled a large scroll. 'May I present Their Royal Highnesses King Hubert and Prince Phillip,' he announced loudly.

King Stefan's face lit up. 'Ah, my old friend,' he murmured to the Queen.

King Hubert bustled into the throne room, followed by his young son, and embraced King Stefan. The two kings were very different – Hubert was as short and round as Stefan was tall and thin – but they had been good friends for many years.

'We have a special gift for your new daughter.' King Hubert beamed. He handed a golden box to his son and gently pushed him towards Aurora's cradle.

Phillip peered in at the baby and pulled a face. Babies are boring, he thought to himself.

King Hubert watched his son bending

over Aurora's cradle and smiled at King Stefan. Phillip didn't know, but both kings had already decided that, when their children were old enough, they would be married. The announcement was to be made this very day...

There was another fanfare of trumpets. Everyone turned to look at a bright, golden sunbeam shining into the castle courtyard. Three glowing sparkles floated in the beam of light. Slowly they changed shape, one by one turning into three plump little fairies.

'Their most Honoured Excellencies, the three good fairies,' announced the herald. 'Mistress Flora, Mistress Fauna and Mistress Merryweather.'

The three fairies wore exactly the same

long dresses, cloaks and pointed hats, but Flora's were orange, Fauna's green and Merryweather's blue. Beaming all over their kind, round faces, they bobbed through the air towards the cradle.

'Oh, the little darling,' Merryweather whispered, peeping in at the baby.

Flora turned to the King and Queen. 'Your Majesties,' she said with a smile, 'each of us the child may bless, with a single gift, no more, no less.' She lifted her wand. 'Little Princess, my gift will be the gift of beauty.' She waved her wand and a shower of flowers fell softly into the cradle.

Then Fauna stepped forward. 'Tiny Princess,' she said, 'my gift will be the gift of song.' With that, sparkling lights drifted down from her wand and into the cradle.

'Sweet Princess,' Merryweather began, 'my gift will be the –'

But the third fairy did not get any further. Suddenly a huge gust of wind howled around the throne room, almost knocking her over. The doors flew open, setting all the banners dancing wildly. Everyone gasped as the hall grew dark. Jagged streaks of silver lightning were followed by a terrifyingly loud crack of thunder.

Green flames began to flicker up from the floor. Higher and higher they grew, twisting and turning, until they formed themselves into a formidable shape. A tall, slender woman dressed in flowing black robes stood before them. She wore a horned headdress and carried a slim cane topped with a golden globe. The woman was very beautiful, but her face was cold and hard and pale. Her presence sent an icy chill through the room.

The three fairies looked anxiously at each other.

'Why, it's Maleficent!' Fauna whispered.

'What does she want here?' Merryweather asked with a frown.

Chapter Two

As everyone stood in silence, a large black raven flew in through the open doors. It came to rest on top of Maleficent's cane.

'Well,' Maleficent purred softly, glancing around the throne room, 'quite a glittering party, King Stefan. Everyone seems to be here. Royalty, nobility...' Her gaze fell on the three fairies standing by the cradle. 'Even the rabble!'

'Ohhh!' Merryweather gasped crossly.

She tried to fly at Maleficent, but Flora pulled her back.

'I really felt quite distressed at not receiving an invitation myself,' Maleficent went on silkily.

'You weren't wanted!' snapped Merryweather.

Maleficent put a hand to her throat, pretending to be embarrassed. 'Not wanted!' she cried. 'Oh dear. What an awkward situation.' There was a tense silence as she stroked the raven's sleek black feathers. 'I had hoped that it was due to some oversight. But in that case, I'd best be on my way.'

'And you're not offended, Your Excellency?' the Queen asked.

A smile twisted Maleficent's mouth.

'Why, no, Your Majesty. And to show that I bear no ill will, I too shall bestow a gift on the child.'

The three fairies gasped in alarm, drawing closer to the cradle.

'Listen well, all of you!' Maleficent proclaimed, striking her cane on the ground. 'The Princess will indeed grow in grace and beauty, and be beloved of all who know her ...'

The King took the Queen's hand. They both looked pale and fearful.

'But before the sun sets on her sixteenth birthday,' Maleficent continued, 'she will prick her finger on the spindle of a spinning wheel and DIE!'

'Oh no!' the Queen cried. She ran over to the cradle and picked up the baby.

'We have a special gift for your daughter.' King Hubert beamed.

'My gift will be the gift of song.' Fauna waved her wand.

'I too shall bestow a gift on the child,' Maleficent said with a twist smile.

The King and Queen watched sadly as the three fairies and Prince Aurora disappeared into the night.

'We want you to go and pick some berries,' said
Merryweather.

'I know you, I walked with you once upon a dream,'
Briar Rose sang.

h had the strangest feeling they had met before.

'Touch the spindle!' Maleficent's voice echoed around the room.

'You fools!' Maleficent hissed. 'Here's your precious Princess!'

uge black dragon breathing yellow fire stood in Maleficent's place.

The Prince bent over the bed and gently kissed her.

'I – I don't understand!' King Hubert stammered

Pointing at Maleficent, King Stefan shouted furiously to the guards, 'Seize that creature!'

However, Maleficent just laughed. 'Stand back, you fools,' she cried, raising her arms.

The sleeves of her robe billowed around her. Lightning flashed and thunder roared. Seconds later Maleficent was swallowed up in a mass of leaping green flames and she vanished from sight.

The throne room was suddenly eerily silent, except for the faint echoes of her evil laughter.

Chapter Three

'Don't despair, Your Majesties,' cried Flora. 'Merryweather still has her gift to give.'

The King looked hopeful. 'Then she can undo this curse?'

'Oh no, Sire,' Merryweather replied.

'Maleficent's powers are far too great,' said Flora.

'But she can help,' Fauna added.

Merryweather waved her wand over the baby's cradle. 'Sweet Princess, if through this wicked witch's trick, a spindle should your finger prick, not in death but just in sleep, this fateful prophecy you'll keep. And from this slumber you'll awake, when true love's kiss the spell shall break.'

Merryweather had done the best she could, but the King and Queen were still terrified that Maleficent's evil spell would harm their beloved daughter. So that very day, King Stefan ordered that every spinning wheel in the kingdom should be brought to the palace and burnt. A huge bonfire blazed in the castle courtyard as the spinning wheels were set alight.

'A bonfire won't stop Maleficent,' remarked Merryweather gloomily.

The three fairies were in the empty

throne room, watching the orange flames leaping up into the night sky.

'Of course not,' Flora agreed.

'Oh, I'd like to turn that Maleficent into a fat old toad!' Merryweather muttered.

'Now, dear,' said Flora, 'you know our magic doesn't work that way. We can bring only joy and happiness.'

'Well, it would make me happy!' Merryweather replied.

'There must be a way,' Flora went on. Then a smile spread across her face. 'Yes! I believe there is!'

'What?' asked Fauna.

'Ssh!' Flora waved her wand, shrinking herself down. 'Even walls have ears. Follow me.'

Flora flew across the room towards the

table where the Princess's christening gifts lay. One of them was a little gold box with two doors. Flora flew into the box, followed by Fauna and Merryweather. The doors closed and the key locked behind them.

'Now, let's see,' Flora said to herself, as Fauna and Merryweather waited impatiently. 'The woodcutter's cottage. No one lives there any more. The King and Queen won't like it, of course. But when we explain it's the only way …'

'Explain what?' asked Merryweather.

'About the three peasant women who will be looking after a baby, deep in the heart of the forest,' Flora replied.

Fauna and Merryweather looked puzzled.

'Who are they?' Merryweather wanted to know.

As Flora waved her wand, Fauna and Merryweather's fairy outfits vanished and they were dressed in simple peasant clothes.

'Why, it's us!' Fauna cried. 'You mean we'll take care of the baby?'

'If humans can do it, so can we,' Flora said firmly.

'And we'll have our magic to help us,' Merryweather added.

'No!' Flora shook her head. 'No magic! Then Maleficent will never suspect what's going on.' She took Fauna's wand. 'And let's get rid of those wings too.'

Meanwhile, Merryweather had backed away, looking worried. 'You mean live like humans for sixteen years?' she gasped, trying to hang on to her wand as Flora took it. 'But we've never done anything without magic!'

'Oh, we'll all pitch in,' Flora assured her. 'Now, we must tell Their Majesties at once!'

As Flora had guessed, the King and Queen were very upset at the thought of their baby being taken away from them. But they also knew that it was the best way of stopping Maleficent's evil curse from coming true.

So late that night, three peasant women stole out of the castle and into the forest. One of them carried a baby in her arms.

The King and Queen watched sadly from the balcony as Flora, Fauna, Merryweather and Princess Aurora disappeared into the night.

Chapter Four

'It's incredible!' cried Maleficent as she stalked around the throne room of her palace on top of the Forbidden Mountain. Her face was pale with fury as she turned on her guards. 'Sixteen years! Sixteen years have passed and not a trace of Princess Aurora anywhere!'

The guards blinked sheepishly.

'She can't have vanished into thin air!' Maleficent snapped. 'Are you sure you've searched everywhere?'

'Yes, everywhere,' mumbled their leader. 'The town, the forest, the mountains. And all the cradles.'

Maleficent turned to face him, her robes swirling around her. 'Cradles?' she repeated.

The leader nodded.

The raven was sitting on the arm of Maleficent's throne. She reached out and stroked the bird's throat. 'Did you hear that, my pet?' she said softly. 'All these years, sixteen long years, they've been looking for –' she glared at the guards – 'a BABY!'

There was a clap of thunder and the guards shrank back.

'Fools!' Maleficent was furious. 'Idiots!' She aimed lightning bolts at the guards, who ran off, tumbling down the stairs in their efforts to get away. Then, sitting down on her throne, she turned and spoke to the raven at her hand. 'You are my last hope. Go and look for a girl of sixteen with hair of sunshine gold.'

The raven flew off through the open window.

'And do not fail me,' Maleficent called after him.

Deep in the heart of the forest was a small woodcutter's cottage. The three fairies had lived here for the past sixteen years, caring for Princess Aurora, whom they had named Briar Rose. Today was her sixteenth birthday.

'We'll make a dress,' Flora decided.

'And a cake,' said Fauna.

'But how are we going to get Briar Rose out of the house?' Merryweather wanted to know.

'What are you three dears up to?' Briar Rose asked, coming downstairs. She was tall, slender and beautiful, with long golden hair.

'We want you to go and pick some berries,' said Merryweather, handing Briar Rose a basket.

'I picked berries yesterday,' Briar Rose began.

'We need more, dear,' said Flora quickly. 'But don't go too far.'

'And don't speak to strangers,' Fauna added.

Smiling, Briar Rose went off into the

forest. As soon as she had gone, Flora opened a trunk and took out a length of pink material, while Fauna hurried into the kitchen.

'I'll get the wands,' said Merryweather, heading for the stairs.

'No magic!' Flora reminded her. 'I'll make the dress.'

'And I'll make the cake,' said Fauna.

Merryweather stared at them. 'But you can't sew and you've never cooked!'

'It's simple,' Flora laughed. 'You can be the dummy, Merryweather!'

Merryweather stood on a stool and Flora wrapped the material round her before she began cutting.

'But it's pink,' Merryweather grumbled.

'I wanted it to be blue.' Then she sighed and tears came to her eyes. 'After today, we won't have any Briar Rose. She'll be a princess again.'

'We've had her for sixteen years,' Flora reminded her, but she too suddenly felt sad.

Meanwhile, Fauna was following the recipe in a cookery book. 'Three cups of flour,' she muttered. 'Two eggs …' And she threw the eggs in, shells and all.

'This looks awful!' Merryweather complained, staring down at the material wrapped round her.

'That's because it's on you, dear,' Flora retorted.

Fauna slapped some icing and candles on top of the cake mixture and stepped back to admire it. 'Well, what do you think?' she asked. 'Oops!' The icing was sliding on to the floor. 'It'll be better when it's baked.'

'I think we've had enough of this nonsense,' Merryweather said in disgust. 'I'm going to get those wands!' And she stomped off upstairs.

'Fauna, close all the windows,' Flora said as Merryweather bounced back downstairs with the wands. 'We can't be too careful. Fauna, you take care of the cake, Merryweather, you clean the room and I'll make the dress.'

The three fairies waved their wands.

Immediately, the bucket, mop and broom sprang into action and began to clean the cottage. Flour, eggs and milk poured themselves into a bowl and began to mix together. Scissors danced about, cutting the pink material into the shape of a beautiful dress.

Merryweather pulled a face. 'Make it blue!' she insisted, flourishing her wand.

'No, pink!' Flora argued, waving her own wand.

Blue and pink sparks flew back and forth as the material changed colour every few seconds. There were so many sparks, some of them flew up the chimney.

Maleficent's raven was soaring high in the sky overhead. He spotted the magical sparks whirling out of the chimney straight away and flew down to take a look.

Chapter Five

Briar Rose walked through the forest, humming to herself and swinging her basket. As she passed by, birds sang in the trees, squirrels peered at her with bright eyes and rabbits popped their heads out of their holes. They were so accustomed to Briar Rose that they weren't scared of her at all.

'I wonder, if my heart keeps singing, will my song go winging, to someone who'll find me?' As Briar Rose sang while she picked berries, her voice echoed through the trees, sweet and clear.

Not far away, Prince Phillip was riding through the forest. Like Briar Rose, he was no longer a child. He was now a tall, handsome young man. He pulled his horse up sharply when he heard the faint, sweet sound and smiled.

'You hear that, Samson?' he said, patting the horse. 'Let's go and find out who it is.'

Briar Rose put her basket down and sighed. 'Oh dear, why do they still treat me like a child?'

'Who-oo?' said an owl, swooping down from the tree.

'My aunts, Flora, Fauna and Merryweather,' Briar Rose explained.

'They never want me to meet anyone.'
She smiled dreamily. 'But in fact I have
met someone. In my dreams. A prince...'

She began to twirl round on the grass,
singing, 'I know you, I walked with you
once upon a dream...'

Suddenly someone was behind her,
gently taking her hands and joining in
the song.

'Oh!' Briar Rose spun round. She saw
a handsome, finely dressed young man.

'Sorry.' Prince Phillip smiled. 'I didn't
mean to frighten you.'

As they stared at each other, both had
the strangest feeling that they had met
somewhere before.

'What's your name?' Phillip asked.

'It's – it's –' Briar Rose stammered,

blushing. 'Oh no, I can't!' And she turned and ran.

'But when will I see you again?' Phillip called anxiously.

'This evening.' Briar Rose smiled to herself as she hurried away. 'At the cottage in the glen.'

Briar Rose wandered home in a happy dream, thinking about the handsome man she had just met. Flora, Fauna and Merryweather were waiting for her. The cottage was spotless, the cake looked delicious and the blue dress was beautiful.

'Happy birthday!' the three fairies chorused.

'Oh!' Briar Rose gasped. 'This is the

happiest day of my life. Everything's so wonderful.' She smiled at the three fairies. 'Just wait until you meet him!' She began to sing. 'Once upon a dream...'

'Him?' Fauna repeated, staring at Briar Rose. 'She's in love!'

'This is terrible!' Flora sighed.

'Why?' Briar Rose looked puzzled.

Fauna took her hands. 'You're already engaged,' she said gently.

'Since the day you were born,' Merryweather added.

'To Prince Phillip, dear,' Fauna explained. Briar Rose's eyes widened. 'But how could I marry a prince?' she asked. 'I'd have to be –'

'A princess,' Merryweather broke in.

'And you are,' Fauna told her.

'Princess Aurora,' said Flora.

Briar Rose looked from one fairy to the other. She couldn't believe what they were saying. None of them noticed Maleficent's raven perched near the open door.

'Tonight we're taking you back to your father, King Stefan,' Flora went on. 'And I'm afraid you must never see that young man again.'

Tears welled up in Briar Rose's eyes. 'Oh no!'

She ran upstairs, leaving the three fairies staring sadly at each other.

Noiselessly, the raven slipped away and flew with haste back to Maleficent's palace.

Chapter Six

The whole kingdom was waiting joyfully for the Princess to return home, but no one was more excited than the King and Queen, who hadn't seen their beloved daughter for sixteen years. King Stefan and Phillip's father, King Hubert, were waiting impatiently for the three fairies to bring Aurora to the castle.

'No sign of her yet,' muttered King Stefan, who was staring anxiously out of the window towards the forest.

'Tonight we toast the future!' Hubert said happily, raising his wine glass. 'Our children will marry and our kingdoms will be united!'

'His Royal Highness, Prince Phillip!' announced a herald, as the young man galloped into the castle courtyard on his horse.

'Phillip!' King Hubert jumped to his feet and dashed down the steps to greet his son. 'Hurry, boy. Go and get changed. You can't meet your future bride looking like that!'

'But I have met her, Father,' cried Phillip, laughing. He grabbed King Hubert and danced around with him. 'Once upon a dream!'

'Now, what's all this dream nonsense?'

his father blustered, straightening his crown.

'It wasn't a dream, Father,' Phillip said, his eyes shining. 'I really did meet her.'

King Hubert looked amazed. 'You met the Princess Aurora?'

'I said I met the girl I am going to marry,' replied Phillip happily. 'I don't know who she is. A peasant girl, maybe.'

'A peasant girl?' King Hubert gasped in horror. 'No, Phillip, you can't do this to me! You're a prince and you're going to marry a princess!'

'You're living in the past, Father,' Phillip said firmly. 'This is the fourteenth century and I'm going to marry the girl I love!' With that, he jumped on Samson's back and galloped off.

'Phillip, stop!' King Hubert called. He shook his head sadly. 'How will I ever tell Stefan?'

Meanwhile, Flora, Fauna and Merryweather were leading Briar Rose through the forest. Not a soul was about as they made their way across the castle courtyard and into the castle. The three fairies took her to a lavishly decorated bedroom, where a fire had been lit to welcome them.

Flora sat Briar Rose down at the dressing table. 'This one last gift, dear child, for thee,' she said softly, 'the symbol of thy royalty.'

The fairies waved their wands. A gold crown studded with sparkling jewels appeared and Flora placed it gently on the Princess's head. Briar Rose stared at herself in the mirror and began to cry.

Flora ushered Fauna and Merryweather out of the room. 'Let her have a few moments to herself,' she whispered.

Left alone, Briar Rose sobbed bitterly. She did not notice that the fire was burning brighter, or that wisps of smoke were rising higher and higher into the air.

The smoke faded, and the evil face and figure of Maleficent glowed briefly at the back of the fireplace. Then she too faded into a bright green wisp of smoke.

Briar Rose looked up and saw the emerald smoke floating in the air. She stood as if in a trance and moved towards it. Strange, haunting music played softly as she headed straight for the fireplace.

Outside, the three fairies were talking in low voices.

'Oh, I don't see why she has to marry a prince!' Merryweather was muttering.

'Listen,' Flora whispered as she heard the music drifting out from the room. 'It's Maleficent!'

Pale with terror, the fairies burst into the room. They were just in time to see the brick wall at the back of the fireplace open up and Briar Rose disappear behind it.

'Rose!' they called, dashing forward to stop her. But it was too late. Just as they reached the opening, the bricks reappeared.

'Rose!' called out Flora, once the fairies had finally moved the wall aside with their magic. 'Rose, where are you?'

Her eyes wide and dazed, Briar Rose followed the glowing green smoke up a circular stairway. At the top of the steps stood an open door and she went inside. The wisp of smoke was hovering in the centre of the room. As she walked towards it, it curled and stretched and formed itself into a spinning wheel. At the top of the wheel was a very long, sharp spindle.

'Rose!' Flora, Fauna and Merryweather were hurrying up the stairs. 'Don't touch anything!'

'Touch the spindle!' Maleficent's voice echoed round the room. 'Touch it, I say!' Briar Rose reached out slowly towards the spindle...

The three fairies rushed into the room and gasped as Maleficent loomed over them.

'You fools!' she hissed. 'Thinking you could defeat me!' She pulled her robes aside. 'Well, here's your precious Princess!'

Chapter Seven

Briar Rose was lying on the floor, her golden hair spread around her. She looked pale and still.

'Oh, Rose!' the three fairies wailed, as Maleficent disappeared in a burst of flames and smoke, her sinister laugh echoing after her.

Meanwhile, the King and Queen were waiting impatiently for their daughter to arrive. The main hall was full of people who had come from all over the kingdom to celebrate. The only person who wasn't happy was King Hubert. He tugged at his friend's arm.

'Er – Stefan, I've got something to tell you,' he muttered, wondering how he was going to break the bad news about Phillip.

'Ssh!' King Stefan hissed, as a herald stepped forward.

'The sun has set,' the herald announced. 'Make ready to welcome the Princess!'

Everyone cheered and colourful fireworks began to explode in the dark sky.

The three fairies had gently placed the sleeping Aurora on the bed and now looked tearfully at one another.

'Poor King Stefan and the Queen,' Fauna said softly.

'They'll be heartbroken when they find out,' Merryweather sniffed.

Flora brushed away a tear. 'They're not going to,' she decided. 'We'll put them all to sleep until Rose awakens!'

Quickly, Flora, Fauna and Merryweather made themselves tiny and flew off around the castle, scattering magic sleep-dust. They began with the guards, who yawned and fell asleep where they stood. Then they moved into the banqueting hall, where people were feasting, and in a few moments everyone was sound asleep there too.

Flora flew over to King Hubert and

King Stefan.

'I've – er – just been talking to Phillip,' Hubert said awkwardly, yawning hugely as Flora scattered her sleep-dust, 'and he's fallen in love with some peasant girl …'

But King Stefan was already asleep and King Hubert's eyes were beginning to droop as well.

Flora's face lit up. 'A peasant girl!' she gasped, and flew straight over to King Hubert. 'Where did he meet her?'

The King opened one eye. 'Once upon a dream,' he yawned, and then he began to snore.

'Rose! Prince Phillip!' Flora cried excitedly. She hurried back to the others. 'We've got to go to the cottage!'

*

As they flew out of the castle and returned to the forest, Flora explained what she had discovered. When the fairies reached the cottage, they were expecting to see Prince Phillip waiting for Briar Rose, but there was no sign of him. The cottage was dark and empty.

'Look!' Flora had spotted something lying on the floor. She swooped down and picked it up. It was a hat with a feather in it. 'Prince Phillip was here.'

'Maleficent!' Merryweather gasped. 'She's got the Prince!'

'At the Forbidden Mountain,' Flora said, with dread in her voice.

'But we can't go there!' Fauna cried.

'We can and we must!' Flora announced firmly.

Chapter Eight

Maleficent's palace stood, dark and gloomy, on top of the tall, black mountain. Flora, Fauna and Merryweather hid behind a rock and peered out, checking for guards. Then they bobbed their way over to the drawbridge.

Suddenly a guard appeared and they whisked themselves back out of sight once more. Next they made themselves into small specks and this time they managed to fly into the castle without being spotted.

The fairies landed on a window-ledge and peeped down into the room. The guards were dancing around a large, blazing fire, while Maleficent sat on her throne, stroking the raven.

'What a pity Prince Phillip can't be here to join in the celebrations,' she purred. 'We must go to the dungeon and cheer him up.'

She rose and walked over to a flight of steps, the raven flying along beside her. Unseen, Flora, Fauna and Merryweather followed. At the bottom of the stairs, in a dark, damp dungeon, sat Prince Phillip, chained to the wall. He looked cold and miserable.

'Oh, come now, Prince Phillip.' Maleficent smiled wickedly. 'Why so sad? In the topmost tower of King Stefan's palace lies the Princess Aurora.' Her smile widened. 'The very same peasant girl you met in the forest! She lies in an ageless sleep. And in one hundred years' time you will be free to leave this dungeon, a grey-haired old man, and ride off to waken your love with love's first kiss!'

Her laughter echoed around the dungeon as Prince Phillip sprang angrily to his feet, straining to break free from his chains.

'You –' Merryweather tried to fly at Maleficent, but the others held her back. The raven turned his head curiously, his bright eyes peering through the darkness.

'A most gratifying day,' Maleficent said with satisfaction, as she and the raven left the dungeon.

Wasting no time, the three fairies flew down from the window-ledge. Prince Phillip's eyes widened in amazement as they shot up to their normal size.

'Ssh!' Flora tapped the shackles on his arms and they fell away. 'No time to explain!'

Fauna did the same to the chains on his ankles, while Merryweather peeked out of the door, checking for guards.

'Arm thyself with this enchanted shield of virtue and this mighty sword of truth.' Flora waved her wand, and a shield and a sword appeared in the Prince's hands. 'Now come, we must hurry.'

They all rushed from the dungeon, but only to come face to face with the raven, which was flying down the stairs.

Chapter Nine

'Caw! Caw!' the raven squawked furiously, and flew back up the stairs to fetch the guards.

Prince Phillip turned and ran the other way, and the fairies bobbed along behind him. They found another staircase and dashed up it as the guards came running towards them. At the top of the stairs was a window. The fairies flew through it and Prince Phillip jumped after them down into the courtyard. Samson, who was chained too, heard his master and whinnied loudly.

'Phillip,' Flora called, as the guards began to hurl boulders from the window, 'watch out!' She waved her wand, turning the boulders into harmless bubbles.

As Merryweather set about burning through Samson's chains with magic, the guards began firing arrows at them. Flora waved her wand again and the arrows turned into flowers that simply fell to the ground.

Prince Phillip urged Samson forward as the raven flapped overhead. The horse raced towards the drawbridge, just as the guards started pouring boiling oil in their path. But Flora was ready with her wand again and turned the oil into a dazzling rainbow.

The raven whirled round and, calling loudly, flew up to the throne room to warn Maleficent. Merryweather followed him. The determined little fairy chased him round and round the tower and, with one whisk of her wand, turned him to stone. Then she flew back to join the others.

'Silence!' Maleficent thundered, stalking out of the tower room. 'Tell those fools to –' Her eyes widened as she realized that her raven had been turned to stone. 'NO!'

Now the castle drawbridge was rising higher and higher as Prince Phillip galloped desperately along it.

'Watch out, Phillip!' Fauna cried.

All three fairies waved their wands, helping Samson to make the giant leap from the rising drawbridge to the rocks beyond.

Furiously, Maleficent rushed to the top of the tower and lifted her cane, her robes billowing in the wind. She hurled a lightning bolt at a stone arch as Phillip rode through it, sheltering beneath his shield. Another lightning bolt hit the rocky ridge and the path crumbled away. Samson and Phillip slid down the side of the cliff, the fairies flying anxiously above them.

'A forest of thorns shall be his tomb,' Maleficent cried, staring at King Stefan's palace in the distance, 'borne through the skies on a fog of doom. Now go with a curse and serve me well. Round Stefan's castle, cast my spell.'

Lightning bolts immediately struck the castle and a great wall of thick thorny branches began to grow, twining upwards to a great height and blocking the Prince's path.

Phillip rode forward, his face determined. He began to hack his way through the thorns as Samson whinnied with fright. Soon he was panting and his hands were cut and bruised, but he did not stop until he had forced a way through to the palace.

Maleficent stared in horror. 'No!' she cried, and instantly vanished in a whirl of purple and gold sparks. A second later flames flared in front of Prince Phillip, and Samson reared up in terror as Maleficent appeared.

'Now you shall deal with me, O Prince,' Maleficent hissed, 'and all the powers of HELL!'

The flames leapt higher and Maleficent shot upwards, becoming taller, her shape changing. Seconds later a huge black dragon breathing yellow fire stood in her place.

As the fairies watched, horrified, the dragon spat a stream of flames at Phillip. He fell off his horse and backed away towards the edge of the cliff. Another blast sent him tumbling over, even closer to the edge. Desperately, he lashed out with his sword at the dragon's head as its long, sharp teeth snapped and snarled. The next blast knocked the shield from the Prince's grasp.

'Ha ha ha!' Maleficent's evil laughter echoed through the flames as the dragon moved in for the kill.

Quickly, the three fairies touched the tip of the Prince's sword with fairy dust.

'Now sword of truth, fly swift and sure,' Flora cried, 'that evil die and good endure!'

Prince Phillip pulled back his arm and hurled the sword with every bit of strength he possessed. It buried itself deep in the dragon's chest. With a cry, the wounded creature stumbled forward, then plunged over the edge to the bottom of the cliff.

Chapter Ten

Prince Phillip hurried through the castle courtyard. He noticed the people standing around, sleeping where they stood, as he headed towards the tower room where Aurora lay.

The three fairies watched happily as he bent over the bed and gently kissed her. Her eyes opened slowly and she smiled as she recognized the Prince. There was no need for any words.

In the rest of the castle, everyone else

began to wake up as well. King Stefan and his Queen opened their eyes. So did King Hubert.

'Now, Hubert, you were saying?' Stefan turned to his friend.

'Well...' King Hubert looked embarrassed. 'To come to the point, my son Phillip says he's going to marry –'

There was a blast of trumpets. As everyone turned, Phillip and Aurora came down the stairs smiling, hand in hand.

'It's Aurora!' King Stefan cried in delight. 'She's here!'

King Hubert rubbed his eyes in disbelief as Aurora ran into her mother's arms. Up on the balcony, the three fairies smiled at each other, tears of happiness in their eyes.

'I – I don't understand!' King Hubert stammered.

Aurora smiled and kissed him on the cheek, and then, as the music began, she danced off across the floor with her Prince.

'Oh, I love happy endings!' Fauna sobbed.

'So do I,' Flora agreed. Then she frowned as she noticed Aurora's blue dress. 'Pink!' she whispered, lifting her wand.

'No, blue!' Merryweather replied, changing the dress back again, as the Prince and Aurora danced on, knowing that now they would live happily ever

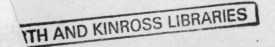